Mouse Finds a House

Written by
Karen Hoenecke

Illustrated by
Laura Lydecker

Chicken, may I come in?
Sorry, mouse. This is not your house.

Pig, may I come in?
Sorry, mouse. This is not your house.

Horse, may I come in?
Sorry, mouse. This is not your house.

Fish, may I come in?
Sorry, mouse. This is not your house.

Robin, may I come in?
Sorry, mouse. This is not your house.

Mouse, may I come in?
Of course. This is a mouse house.